Helen at Home and the Letter H

Alphabet Friends

by *Cynthia Klingel and Robert B. Noyed*

The **Child's World**®

The **Child's World**®

Published in the United States of America
by The Child's World®
P.O. Box 326
Chanhassen, MN 55317-0326
800-599-READ
www.childsworld.com

The Child's World®: Mary Berendes, Publishing Director

Editorial Directions, Inc.: E. Russell Primm, Editorial
Director; Emily Dolbear, Line Editor; Ruth Martin,
Editorial Assistant; Linda S. Koutris, Photo Researcher
and Selector

Photographs ©: Thinkstock/Getty Images: Cover & 9, 21;
Spencer Grant/PhotoEdit: 10; Jose Luis Pelaez, Inc./
Corbis: 13; Corbis 14, 18; Kevin R. Morris/Corbis: 17.

Library of Congress Cataloging-in-Publication Data
Klingel, Cynthia Fitterer.
   Helen at home and the letter H / by Cynthia Klingel
and Robert B. Noyed.
      p. cm. — (Alphabet readers)
Summary: A simple story about what a girl named
Helen does when she has the house all to herself
introduces the letter "h".
   ISBN 1-59296-098-7 (alk. paper)
   [1. Play--Fiction. 2. Alphabet.] I. Noyed, Robert B. II.
Title. III. Series.
   PZ7.K6798He 2003
   [E]—dc21   2003006534

Note to parents and educators:
The first skill children acquire before becoming successful readers is individual letter recognition. The Alphabet Friends series has been created with the needs of young learners in mind. Each engaging book begins by showing the difference between the capital letter and the lowercase letter. In each of the books on the vowels and the consonants c and g, children are introduced to the different sounds that the letter can make. Finally, children see that the letters can be found at the beginning of a word, in the middle of a word, and in most cases, at the end of a word.

Following the introduction, children meet their Alphabet Friends. The friend in each story encounters many words that include the featured letter of that book. Each noun that begins with the title letter is highlighted in red with the initial letter of the word in bold. Above the word is a rebus drawing that establishes a strong picture cue.

At the end of each book, we have included three words lists. Can your young learners find all the words in each book with the title letter in them?

Let's learn about the letter **H.**

The letter **H** can look like this: **H.**

The letter **H** can also look like this: **h.**

The letter **h** can be at the beginning of a word, like hand.

hand

The letter **h** can be in the middle of a word, like feather.

feat**h**er

The letter **h** can be at the
end of a word, like fish.

fis**h**

Helen is happy. She has the house to

herself. Her sister is visiting a friend.

Her mom is busy working downstairs.

How will she spend her day?

Helen's hamster wants to play. Helen

holds the hamster in her hands. Hang

on to her, Helen!

Helen helps her **h**amster back into the

cage. She does not want anything to

happen to the **h**amster.

Helen decides to play her sister's

horn. She blows hard into the **h**orn.

The **h**orn honks and hoots.

Helen hurries down the **h**all to her

mother's room. She brushes her **h**air.

She puts on a **h**at. She has an idea.

Helen will have a party! She wishes

her sister could be at her party. But

she's not supposed to be back for an

hour. **H**elen hears a sound.

Her sister has come home early. "Hello,

Helen. I'm **h**ome!" **H**elen is happy to

have someone else come to her party!

Fun Facts

All mammals have hair. Even a porcupine's quills are hair! Mammals are also the only living things that have hair. Hair helps mammals in different ways. Hair keeps some mammals warm. The color of hair can help an animal blend into its environment and hide from enemies. Humans mostly use their hair to look good!

Do you know anyone who has a hamster? Hamsters are small, furry animals often kept as pets. They are mostly active during the night. The largest hamsters are about 12 inches (30 centimeters) long. Some kinds are as small as 2 inches (5.3 cm) long. There are about 15 different kinds of hamsters, and 8 kinds are kept as pets.

Horn is the name for a group of musical instruments. Some horn instruments include the bugle, trombone, trumpet, tuba, and French horn. Helen's sister's horn is a trumpet. Trumpets have been around for more than 3,000 years!

To Read More

About the Letter H

Flanagan, Alice K. *Hats Can Help: The Sound of H*. Chanhassen, Minn. The Child's World, 2000.

About Hair

Parr, Todd. *This Is My Hair*. Boston: Little, Brown, 1999.

Wilhelm, Hans. *Don't Cut My Hair*. New York: Scholastic, 1997.

About Hamsters

Suen, Anastasia and Allen Eitzen (illustrator). *Hamster Chase*. New York: Viking, 2001.

Watts, Barrie. *Hamster*. Morristown, N.J.: Silver Burdett Co., 1986.

About Horns

Temple, Bob. *Trombones*. Chanhassen, Minn.: The Child's World, 2003.

Temple, Bob. *Tubas*. Chanhassen, Minn.: The Child's World, 2003.

Words with H

Words with H at the Beginning
hair
hall
hamster
hand
hands
hang
happen
happy
hard
has
hat
have
hears
Helen
Helen's
hello
helps
her
herself
holds
home
honks
hoots
horn
hour
house
how
hurries

Words with H in the Middle
anything
brushes
feather
mother's
she
the
this
wishes

Words with H at the End
fish

About the Authors

Cynthia Klingel has worked as a high school English teacher and an elementary teacher. She is currently the curriculum director for a Minnesota school district. Cynthia Klingel lives with her family in Mankato, Minnesota.

Robert B. Noyed started his career as a newspaper reporter. Since then, he has worked in communications and public relations for a Minnesota school district for more than fourteen years. Robert B. Noyed lives with his family in Brooklyn Center, Minnesota.